Leo Lizard's
Classroom
Adventure

ISBN 978-1-64258-737-1 (paperback)
ISBN 978-1-64258-738-8 (digital)

Christian Faith Publishing, Inc.
832 Park Avenue
Meadville, PA 16335
www.christianfaithpublishing.com

Printed in the United States of America

Leo Lizard's
Classroom Adventure

Lisa Lauro

It was a beautifully hot spring day when Leo Lizard set out to find his friend, Lily. The weather had been rather cool the past few days, and Leo hadn't had much time to play with his friends. His mom always insisted that he stay indoors on chilly days, for fear that he would catch a cold. Before Leo left his home, his mom reminded him to be back in time for dinner and to keep an eye on the sky as afternoon thunderstorms were in the forecast.

Leo ran over to the huge palm tree next to the schoolyard where his best friend, Lily, lived. He whistled to Lily using their secret code for calling each other. Leo had a very high-pitched whistle for a lizard. Suddenly, Lily scurried from behind a rock at the bottom of the palm tree. Delighted to see her friend, Lily gave Leo a huge toothy grin. She was thrilled to have someone to play with, and the two lizards decided to play in the sun for the afternoon.

Their favorite game was Hide and Seek. Leo and Lily took turns hiding for hours. Just as Mama figured, Leo forgot to check the sky for the impending afternoon storm. Sure enough, gray clouds rolled in slowly until the blue skies disappeared, and darkness began to loom over the schoolyard.

It was Leo's turn to seek out Lily when out of nowhere, a loud crack of thunder shook the ground.

BOOOOOOM!

Leo, who is petrified of thunder, darted as fast as he could toward the school. He ran so fast right through the slight opening at the bottom of the metal blue school door.

In a moment's time, Leo realized what he had done. He ran from a scary thunderstorm to an even scarier place… a classroom full of second graders! The room was full of kids, and they were everywhere. Some were working at their desks; others were talking to the teacher, and one little boy with blond hair and a blue shirt was just getting out of the bathroom. Leo was panting so hard he could barely catch his breath, but this was no time to take a breather. He had to find a place to hide and quickly.

Leo hoped that he hadn't been noticed as he slithered in between desks and chairs toward the back of the room. He found a quiet place beside a book bag lying on the floor. Thankfully, the bag was a dark greenish-brown color, and it camouflaged him well. He had to take a deep breath and think about how he would ever get out of this classroom without getting stepped on or caught!

Suddenly, Tommy, the little boy with the blond hair and blue shirt, screamed at the top of his lungs, "There's a lizard in the classroom!" Just then, everything in the room seemed to stop. It was perfectly quiet and still as Tommy seemed to get everyone's attention at once. All the kids began to look around for Leo as if they had special antennae on their heads that detected lizards!

Mrs. Zippay, the teacher, said to the class, "It's time for art. Please get your art shirts and line up quickly and quietly at the front door."

As Mrs. Zippay's class left the room to go to art class, Leo sighed with relief. The thunder was still rumbling outside, and the lightning was fierce. Leo thought about Lily and hoped that wherever she was hiding, she was safe. Leo did remember that Lily was very brave, and these types of thunderstorms never seemed to affect her. He had hoped that Lily would forgive him for running away and leaving her without saying goodbye.

Now that the room was cleared out, Leo thought that he'd better look around for a better place to settle down in case the storm lasted a while. As he crept slowly out from beneath the book bag, he scanned the room. Out of the corner of his eye, just above his head, there was a tree with large green leaves, some grass, and a vine. *How could this be?* Leo thought. Leo hurried as he climbed up a chair and across the counter to the grass at the bottom of the board. "Wow, it's a forest!" cried Leo. At last, Leo had found the perfect place to rest and ride out the storm.

As Leo made himself comfortable in the grass beneath a large leaf, he thought of his mama. He knew that she would be worried sick about him. She knew her son was scared silly of storms. He hoped that she too would forgive him for worrying her. Now, if only the kids in Mrs. Zippay's class wouldn't see him, he might just make it out alive by the end of the day. With that thought, Leo fell fast asleep to the buzz of the fluorescent lights up above him.

At the end of art, Mrs. Zippay's class returned to the classroom. One by one, they filed in the room talking about the lightning that just flashed while they were walking through the breezeway. Johnny—a short, thin boy with brown hair and green eyes—was telling Mrs. Zippay all about his drawing he made during art when Tommy banged his hand on the desk.

BANG BANG BANG!

Tommy shouted, "Hey you, lizard, I hope you're not hiding in my desk because when I get my hands on you, you're…"

Just then, Leo woke to all the noise and confusion in the classroom. He was so startled from Tommy and his banging, he fell right off the cozy green leaf and into the grass below. He was dazed for a minute until he realized where he was.

Leo peeked out from the bulletin-board grass to hear Mrs. Zippay informing the class of their homework assignment. She called them row by row to pack their bags and sit quietly on the carpet until the bell rang for dismissal.

As he waited for the bell to ring, Leo looked out the window to see if he could see Lily outside in the yard. A second later, he saw Lily scurry toward the rock beside her home in the palm tree. "Phew," Leo sighed to himself. "Lily is back home safely." As he was peering out the window, he also noticed that the rain slowed down to a drizzle, and the sounds of thunder were far off in the distance. *Wow, I must have been sleeping a while,* thought Leo.

After pondering, he admitted to himself that although Mrs. Zippay's class was noisy and scary, he had the deepest restful sleep ever! Had he not been afraid of getting caught by Tommy or the others, he would consider returning to his serene hideout another day soon!

RIIING went the bell; it nearly gave Leo a heart attack. He was shaking so badly he could see the grass moving beside him. His eyes bulged out of his head, and he screamed uncontrollably.

"Ahhh!" he shouted. Thankfully, the sound of the bell drowned out Leo's scream, or he would have given himself away for sure! Leo thought his ears were blown out for a second as every noise seemed to echo and ring in his eardrums.

As soon as the last kid in Mrs. Zippay's class left for the day, Leo scurried across the counter, down the chairs, and out the door. Leo ran straight home to his mom who was pacing back and forth, waiting anxiously for Leo to return.

Leo ran through the front door and yelled for his mom. "I'm home!"

"Oh, Leo," cried his mom. Where have you been?"

She explained to Leo that she was worried sick about him.

Leo said, "I'm very sorry that I worried you, Mom, but you are never going to believe the day that I have had." And for the next hour, Leo told his mom all about his day in Mrs. Zippay's class, and he even told her that he would love to go to school one day too!

About the Author

I am a school teacher. I have been teaching in the primary grades for most of my career. My grandmother and sister were also teachers and inspired me to be an educator. I love to read books, write and do artwork during my free time. I reside in Florida with my daughter. I also enjoy going to the beach and traveling to new places.

CPSIA information can be obtained
at www.ICGtesting.com
Printed in the USA
BVHW021128240219
541026BV00018B/593/P

9 781642 587371